Alpharetta, Georgia

Copyright © 2024 by Brycelyn Chavis

All rights reserved. No part of this book may be reproduced or transmitted in any form or by any means, electronic or mechanical, including photocopying, recording, or any information storage and retrieval system, without permission in writing from the author.

ISBN: 978-1-6653-0868-7

∞ This paper meets the requirements of ANSI/NISO Z39.48-1992 (Permanence of Paper)

070124

Pop has a secret.
Pop can't run, Pop can't jump and
Pop can't hop anymore because...

Pop has Parkinson's.

Do you know someone special with Parkinson's?

Draw/add your special person

This is my special

———————

I love them so much!

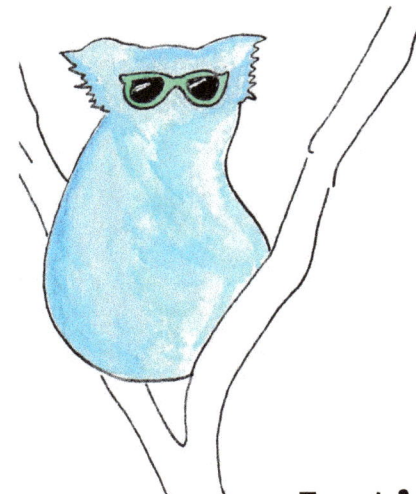

Let's follow these mystery characters to learn how Parkinson's makes Pop feel.

Your special person might want you to know that's how they're feeling too!

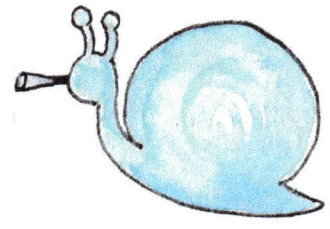

During the day, Pop often drifts away to sleep even when it's not bedtime.

Pop's long naps allow him to rest and dream about the things that make him happy!

These days Pop takes his time getting around. Sometimes his feet shuffle, and he needs you to be patient.

Pop knows he's pretty slow. He wishes he had turbo speed to keep up with you and all the fun!

Occasionally, Pop gets shaky and worries others will stare.

Pop is tough and tries hard to freeze until people look away!

When Pop is not feeling well, he stays tucked away in his room.

Pop would much rather spend his days outdoors, especially near the water!

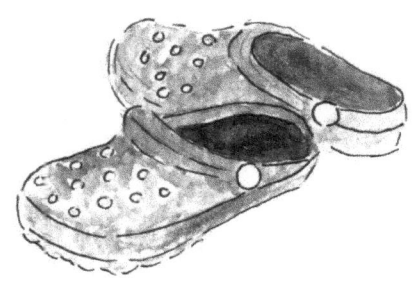

If Pop is frustrated, little things often upset him.

Pop is quickly embarrassed by his behavior and hopes you can forgive him!

Pop isn't able to run, jump, or hop anymore, but he would if he could!

Add your special person's name below.

Although _____ may have lost some of their superpowers, one thing that will never change is how much _____ loves you!

a note for grown-ups:

Instead of wishing things were different, I hope this book encourages you and your family to accept the decline and cherish the time you have with your special person.

tiny takeaways:

💗 Check in often: a call, a text, a card, or even a treat
💗 Be patient and calm when they get frustrated
💗 Give a smile instead of a stare
💗 Know they love you even when they are grumpy
💗 Talk about happy times and fun memories
💗 Listen

This book is dedicated to every person who loved my dad.

Thank you.

Printed in the USA
CPSIA information can be obtained
at www.ICGtesting.com
LVHW070200140924
791002LV00023B/339